REDWORLD

Redworld is published by
Stone Arch Books, A Capstone Imprint
1710 Roe Crest Drive
North Mankato, Minnesota 56003
www.mycapstone.com

Library of Congress Cataloging-in-Publication Data
Names: Collins, A. L. (Ai Lynn), 1964– author. | Tikulin, Tomislav, illustrator.
Title: Outcry: defenders of Mars / by A.L. Collins; illustrated by Tomislav Tikulin.
Description: North Mankato, Minnesota: Stone Arch Books, a Capstone imprint, [2018] |
    Series: Sci-finity. Redworld |
Summary: Belle Song and her friends are on a seventh-grade camping trip to
    Mount Olympus, and when Belle injures her leg it turns out that she has
    discovered a rare and valuable mineral used to make space travel more efficient.
    The BAMCorp company claims that the mineral belongs to them, but mining it
    could poison Mars' precious water supply. Soon tensions rise between the
    company officials and protestors who are trying to protect the environment.
Identifiers: LCCN 2017035491 | ISBN 9781496558879 (library binding) | ISBN 9781496558916 (ebook)
Subjects: LCSH: Camping injuries—Juvenile fiction. | Mines and mineral resources—
    Juvenile fiction. | Mineral industries—Environmental aspects—Juvenile fiction. |
    Environmental degradation—Juvenile fiction. | Water-supply—Juvenile fiction. |
    Protest movements—Juvenile fiction. | Science fiction. | Mars (Planet)—Juvenile fiction. |
    CYAC: Science fiction. | Camping—Fiction. | Wounds and injuries—Fiction. | Mines and
    mineral resources—Fiction. | Environmental degradation—Fiction. | Water supply—Fiction. |
    Protest movements—Fiction. | Mars (Planet)—Fiction. | LCGFT: Science fiction.
Classification: LCC PZ7.1.C6447 Ou 2018 | DDC 813.6 [Fic]—dc23
LC record available at https://lccn.loc.gov/2017035491

Editor: Aaron J. Sautter
Designer: Ted Williams
Production: Kathy McColley

Printed and bound in Canada.
010789S18

OUTCRY
DEFENDERS OF MARS

BY A.L. COLLINS
ILLUSTRATED BY TOMISLAV TIKULIN

STONE ARCH BOOKS
a capstone imprint

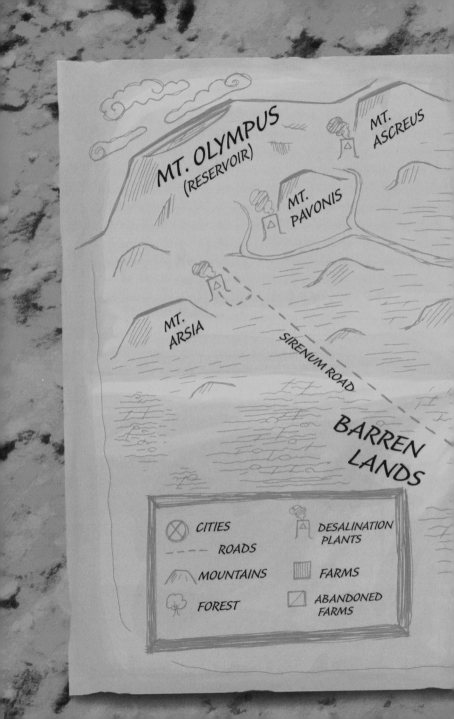

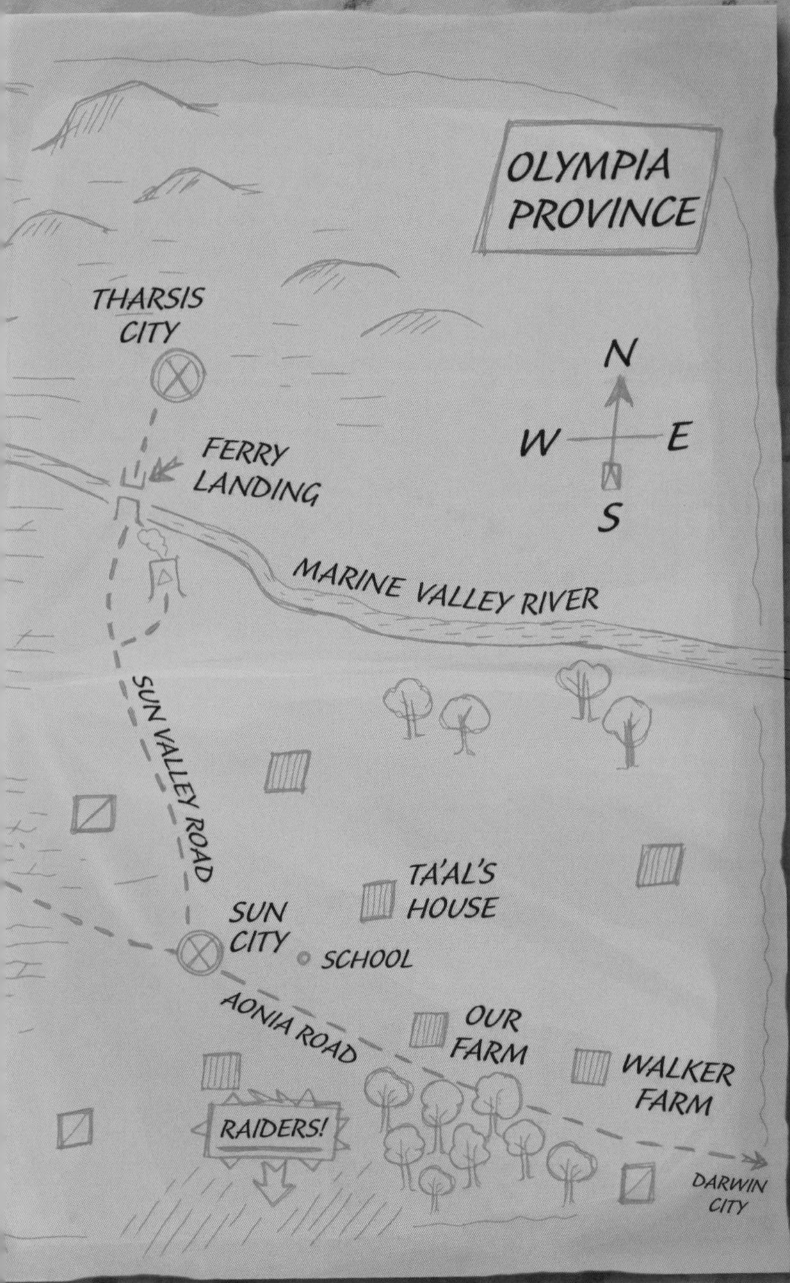
OLYMPIA PROVINCE
THARSIS CITY
N
W
E
S
FERRY LANDING
MARINE VALLEY RIVER
SUN VALLEY ROAD
TA'AL'S HOUSE
SUN CITY
SCHOOL
AONIA ROAD
OUR FARM
WALKER FARM
RAIDERS!
DARWIN CITY

Belle Song
Fourteen-year-old Belle can be headstrong and stubborn. Her curiosity and sense of adventure often get her into trouble. Still, she has a good heart and is passionate about fairness. She is fiercely loyal to her friends.

Yun and Zara Song
Belle's parents sometimes seem really strict. But Yun has a great sense of humor, which Belle both loves and is embarrassed by. Zara has a generous heart, which has taught Belle not to judge others too quickly.

Melody
Melody is an old model 3X Personal Home Helper android. She was given to Belle by her grandmother before she passed away. Melody is Belle's best friend and protector and enjoys telling bad jokes to seem more human.

MAIN INHABITANTS

Lucas Walker
Lucas is Belle's neighbor and classmate. He is part Sulux and part human. Meeting new people is not easy for him. But once he knows someone, his adventurous side emerges. He is full of ideas, which sometimes gets him and his friends into trouble.

Ta'al
Ta'al and her family are Nabian, an ancient alien race from another star system. Born and raised on Mars, Ta'al is intelligent and curious. She enjoys exploring and adventure and quickly becomes Belle's closest friend on Mars.

Raider
Raider is a hybrid wolf-dog. These animals were bred to be tame pets, but some of them became wild. After Raider is rescued by Belle, he becomes a faithful and protective companion.

It is the year 2337. Life on Earth is very difficult. Widespread disease, a lack of resources, and a long war against intelligent robots has caused much suffering. Some Terrans, those who are from Earth, have moved to the Lunar Colony in search of a better life. But the Moon is overcrowded and has limited resources. Other families have chosen to move to Mars instead. With the help of two alien races – the Sulux and the Nabians – the red planet was transformed to support life nearly 200 years ago.

Yun and Zara Song and their daughter, Belle, moved to Mars a little more than one Mars Cycle ago to get a fresh start in life. Here they live as farmers. They work hard to grow crops and raise hybrid animals that are suitable for life on Mars.

Belle is excited to be traveling with her class on her first real trip away from her parents. But while exploring a small cave, she badly injures her leg. In doing so, she discovers a deposit of an incredibly valuable element. Soon Belle and her friends find themselves in the middle of a disagreement about the rare mineral – one that may endanger the future of all who live on . . .

REDWORLD

CHAPTER ONE
:COMPROMISES:

"I can't believe it . . . four whole days with no parents!" Belle laughed, stepping off the shuttle's ramp into the bright sunlight. Her best friend, Ta'al followed close behind. Their shuttle had just landed in the small town of Pettit, in the shadow of Mount Olympus, the largest volcano in the entire Solar System.

Ms. Polley's seventh-grade class was on their first field trip of the year. They were headed for a campground at the base of the towering volcano. Belle and her six classmates were excited to spend the next few days away from their usual routines of farm chores and homework.

Pettit was a town much like Sun City, the town closest to Belle's farm. There was one main street with stores on both sides. Martian-born humans and various aliens hurried past Belle and her friends, ducking in and out of stores and looking very busy.

"Pettit was originally built to house Nabian farmers," Melody informed the class. She was in her teacher mode. "But over the years, it has attracted many different beings. The soil here is especially rich, an important factor for farmers. It is quite a bustling town today."

Belle's android, and oldest friend, had been asked to come along on the trip as an extra helper for Ms. Polley. None of the parents could leave their farms. It was a demanding time for farmers. Many had begun harvesting their crops and few parents had the free time to help.

"Pettit was also one of the first towns to integrate several alien races and humans successfully," Ta'al added. Belle could hear the irritation in her friend's voice. She knew that Ta'al was frustrated that some places on Mars still felt that aliens weren't trusted or welcome.

Belle gave her friend's arm a friendly squeeze. "We're going to have the best camping trip ever!"

Belle could hardly contain her excitement. Back on Earth, her parents thought she was too young to travel on her own. But now that she was fourteen, they couldn't say no. She didn't even mind that they had asked her to take Melody along. She made her android promise to limit her communications back home, however. She longed for her independence and didn't want Melody to report her every movement back to her parents.

"Melody and I will go and settle the hover-wagon rental," Ms. Polley said. "Why don't you kids pick up whatever supplies you might need in that store?" She pointed to the large building with the sign Kru'tar's General Store above the door.

"My parents gave me extra credits to spend on whatever I want," Lucas bragged as they raced to the store.

"My parents didn't bother," Ava, their newest classmate, said. "I have my own account, and it's accepted all over Mars. I only have to give my handprint, and I can buy whatever I want."

Belle looked at Ta'al. Neither of them had that kind of spending power. Both their parents were very careful with their credits. They stepped into the store, admiring the aisles stocked full of goods. This store was bigger than even the biggest store in Sun City.

"They must sell everything," Brill said. He raced up and down the first two aisles, as if the store was the most exciting place in the world.

"This whole aisle is stocked with all kinds of water," Trina added. "There's special spring water, water with minerals to help keep you young, and even water with added flavors."

She and Pavish bought a bottle of fruit-flavored water with added minerals for strength and stamina.

"We'll need this for hiking," Pavish said.

Belle and Ta'al walked quietly through the aisles, trying to decide what to buy.

"I don't really need anything," Belle said. "Melody packed everything we could possibly need."

"Neither do I," Ta'al said. "But I think we can afford to treat ourselves to a packet of Space Rocks candy. They're *suemi* — delicious! We can share it."

"*Sia-mi, sia carnti*," Belle replied using her best Nabian pronunciation.

As the class emerged from the store, Ms. Polley and Melody met them by the rented hover-wagon on the other side of the street. Belle gasped at the sight of their land transport. Her family's wagon at home was at least

ten generations behind this one. This wagon was twice as large and had many features that Belle didn't know even existed in a transport. Like Ta'al's family's wagon, this one didn't need a horsel to pull it. It had its own solar-engine.

"All aboard," Melody said with a swing of her arm. A door opened at the back of the wagon, and a ramp slowly extended outward like a lazy tongue. "We have to hurry if we want to make it to the plant on time."

"What plant?" Lucas asked, climbing into the transport. He slid into a seat by the small dining table.

"We agreed, remember?" Belle said, sitting across from him. "We're stopping by the desalination plant on the way to the campsite."

"Yes," Ta'al said. "It's the largest one in Olympia." She went to explore the guidance controls at the front.

"Actually, I read that it's the biggest one on Mars," Belle corrected.

"Why does that matter?" Ava asked.

Belle's eyes bulged. "Because water matters on Mars, Ava." How her friend didn't know this astounded her.

Ava gave Belle a pouty look. "I know that water matters. But why do we care about getting to the plant?"

Ms. Polley was the last to enter the wagon. Melody pressed the controls to shut the door.

"I believe you were absent the day we discussed touring the plant, Ava," Ms. Polley said. "We even voted on it."

"It was a tie," Pavish said, scrunching up his face.

"That's correct," Ms. Polley said. "And I broke the tie. I think it's an excellent idea to visit the desalination plant. It will be an incredible sight, and educational too."

"They have a marvelous museum there as well," Melody added.

Belle couldn't wait to get there. She had missed out on her opportunity to visit a desalination plant last year. She wasn't going to miss this one for anything. Even Ta'al's face lit up at the prospect of the museum. Nobody else seemed as enthusiastic though.

"I was hoping we could stop by this place," Ava said, holding out her comm device. People used these electronic devices for sending messages and searching for information. A holo-screen popped up on Ava's device, showing the front of a restaurant. It was called The Sweet Life. Below that were more images of a variety of colorful glazed cakes, puddings, and unusual desserts. "It has great ratings on MarsSpoon."

Pavish, Trina, and Brill all cheered at the idea of dessert. Lucas' face went from light purple to bright red. He looked at Belle and then back at the others. Belle knew he was conflicted.

"But we agreed," Belle said. She didn't like it when plans changed at the last minute. And she had looked forward to the plant tour. "We can have dessert any time."

"But I'm hungry now," Pavish said.

"Why don't we vote again?" suggested Ava.

"No!" Belle knew she would lose. Especially since Ava was showing more close-up images of the yummy-looking desserts. "That's not fair!"

"I agree with Belle," Ta'al said quietly. "We already agreed to tour the plant."

The discussion grew into a shouting match. Most of the class wanted dessert. Only Belle and Ta'al were pulling for the plant tour.

"That's quite enough," Ms. Polley finally said, swiveling the driver's seat to face them. She leaned her elbows on her lap, and her thick eyebrows knit together tightly. "Maybe there's a way to reach a compromise."

"A what?" Lucas said. He'd been arguing to go to The Sweet Life, but he looked guilty doing it.

"A compromise is when two sides that don't agree on something each choose to give up something to reach an agreement." Now Ms. Polley using her teacher voice.

The classmates were quiet for a while as they thought it over.

"There's a shorter version of the tour that starts an hour later than the full tour," Belle said, studying the plant website on her datapad. She wasn't happy about it, but she knew this was the only way she'd get to see the plant. If her classmates had their way, they wouldn't stop there at all. "And the museum is open late," she finished.

Ava's mouth twisted to one side. "We could get our desserts to go," she suggested.

"Yeah! This is a great dining table," Lucas said, looking a little relieved. "It expands. See?" He pulled at a lever and the table grew to twice its size. "We could travel and eat at the same time."

The others agreed.

"I don't care," Pavish said. "As long as I get to eat."

"Thank you everyone. This is a great example of a good compromise," Ms. Polley said, looking pleased. She turned back to the wagon's computer and entered the coordinates for the restaurant first, followed by the desalination plant.

Melody took her place at the front as the "co-pilot," as she called it. Everyone found a seat, and they were off.

Sol 48, Autumn/Cycle 106
Late afternoon.

Dessert was nice. Actually — it was amazing!
The restaurant was owned by a Sulux family.
They make desserts from all over the galaxy. I had
something from a planet whose name I can't even
pronounce. But it was SO good. It was colorful,
smooth, and creamy. And it fizzled and popped as
I ate it. It was an entire experience!

We got to the plant just in time for the short
tour. The others won't admit it, but I know they
enjoyed the tour. The guide was so clever, she made
a game out of the tour to keep everyone entertained.

At the museum, we picked up some bottles that
can purify stream water. These will be useful for
camping. We also downloaded the maps we'll need.

But the biggest lesson we learned was that we
must be careful to save our water and not waste it.
We also have to work to keep our water sources pure
and clean. We learned a lot of good lessons. Like the
guide said — we are the future of this planet.
We should take care of it.

I can't wait until we get to the campsite!
Ms. Polley says it'll be another hour or so.

CHAPTER TWO
A FORK IN THE TRAIL

"We're here!" Ms. Polley announced. She got out
to register their group at the campground entrance and
let Melody guide the hover-wagon through the gate.

Belle shut down the book that she and Ta'al
were reading. The holo-screen fizzled into nothing.
The others had fallen asleep after the tour, and were
stretching noisily now.

Melody piloted the wagon to their assigned spot and hit the switch to open the back door. The ramp rumbled to the ground. Belle and Ta'al were the first to rush outside. Belle took a deep breath.

"Ah! Fresh mountain air," she said with a huge smile.

"Indeed," Melody said, handing Belle her pack. "This mountain goes up to twenty-five kilometers in altitude."

"I wonder what the air is like all the way at the top?" Lucas said as he dragged his backpack out of the wagon.

"Very few people have reached the top," Ta'al said. Her pack cleverly floated off the ground. It had an anti-gravity function. "And none were human."

Ms. Polley piled supplies into Melody's arms. The android carried them to the middle of the campsite.

"Never mind," Ms. Polley said. "We're here to study the plants and wildlife, not climb the mountain."

The entire campground was surrounded by thick forest. Thousands of tall trees swayed gently in the mountain breeze. The class' own little campsite was in a small clearing encircled by trees. The forest was so thick that they couldn't see their neighbors, or if there even were any. The air was sweet and cool, and the only sound, aside from the kids' chattering, was the chirping of birds and the occasional creak of a branch high up in a tree.

Everyone helped to set up camp. Soon four tents were pitched and a shelter was put up to house the kitchen and dining area. Belle and Ta'al were sharing a tent. Ava shared with Trina, and the three boys got to use the extra-large tent. Ms. Polley got a small one all to herself. Melody would charge herself inside the hover-wagon. That was the safest place for the android.

As everyone unpacked, Melody prepared to make a fire in the stone pit right in the middle of the camp. She arranged a stack of wood in the pit, and then pulled out a long, thin stick from a storage compartment in her torso.

"This is called a matchstick," she said, holding it up for everyone to see. The whole class had gathered to watch her build the fire. "We are doing this camping activity the old, old, old-fashioned way. I have done all the research."

Belle heard the others groan.

"Why can't we just use a thermowisp?" Ava whispered to Trina. "It's so much faster and the heat spreads evenly all around."

"She's trying to be 'all natural'," Trina whispered back. "Isn't that what she said in the wagon?"

Belle felt bad for her android friend.

"That's a wonderful idea," Belle said, even as she saw her friends frown and scrunch their noses in doubt.

Melody used several matches, but the wood didn't seem to want to burn. After several minutes, the students were about to ask Melody to give up. They thought the usual ion-heaters would be better. But then small tongues of fire peeked out from beneath the tented sticks.

Within minutes, the seven classmates were gathered around a blazing fire. They took turns blowing the smoke into each other's faces as the breeze changed direction. Meanwhile, Melody brought them all drinks and snacks.

"I don't want to smell like smoke," Ava exclaimed whenever the smoke floated in her direction.

"Then you shouldn't have come camping," said Brill.

"It can't be helped," Belle said. "Back on Earth my family went camping every year. We always smelled like smoke afterward."

Ava disappeared into her tent, stomping all the way there. The others just laughed.

"I think we should go for a walk," Ms. Polley said, emerging from her tiny tent. "Let's leave Melody to prepare the evening meal in peace."

Ms. Polley had tied her thick curls into a bun on top of her head. She held a hat in one hand and carried a backpack in the other. She also wore a coat that was full of pockets. Belle couldn't resist counting them.

"Every one of those eight pockets is stuffed with things," Belle whispered to Ta'al, giggling. "She's probably prepared for any emergency, including an alien invasion."

"Very resourceful," Ta'al said. Belle looked at her. That wasn't a joke. Ta'al truly admired their teacher's choice in clothing.

The class followed Ms. Polley to the trailhead. She insisted that they each carry along a small pack. There was a sign at the trail entrance that held a map showing the various paths that could be taken. One path had a big red X mark over it. Under the mark were the words *Under Construction, No Access.*

"We'll take the easiest trail to start off," Ms. Polley said, pointing to the path on the map that was lit up in green. "I want you to each take note of one plant. Take a holo-image of it, and then we'll look them up and learn something new about them. But don't pluck any of the plants. We want to leave nature as we found it."

The boys groaned.

"I thought this was a vacation," Ava piped up from the back. "Why are we doing homework?"

"It's not homework," Ms. Polley said, looking ahead at the path. "We're learning about the world we live in, so we know how to preserve it."

Under
Construction,
No Access.

"Or improve it," Ta'al added.

"Agreed, Ta'al," Ms. Polley said. "Come along." She picked up her pace and marched into the forest.

Belle and Ta'al kept pace with their teacher while the others ambled along behind. Belle would point out interesting plants, and Ta'al would record them.

The path took them on a mild slant upward. The forest was dense and not much light got through the thick canopy. So even though they were warmed by their own exercise, the air felt chilly. Belle was glad that Ms. Polley had made them pack a light coat in their bags. She didn't need it yet, but she was glad it was there if she did.

On several occasions, the path forced them to turn sharply. Ms. Polley called that a switchback. It usually happened when the slope became steep. After the tenth switchback, Belle was panting heavily. She wasn't as fit as she thought she was. Looking back at her friends, she saw that they were getting tired too.

"Ms. Polley, can we take a break?" Belle called to her teacher. "We could all use some water."

"That's fine," Ms. Polley replied, looking at her comm device. "You all rest for a few minutes while I go ahead. I'm trying to get a signal to Melody so she won't worry that we're running late. Stay right here. I won't be far."

Belle sat down and pulled out her water bottle. Ta'al joined her, while Ms. Polley continued on. The others pulled out their bottles too and gulped thirstily.

"Ms. Polley's like a machine!" Lucas said, gasping. "Doesn't she ever get tired?"

"I haven't got a holo-image of any plants yet," Ava complained. "Ms. Polley is going too fast."

Belle pointed out a fern-like plant to her side. "There," she said. "Take an image of that."

"That's a very common plant," Ta'al whispered to Belle. "We have those at home."

"Ms. Polley didn't say it had to be unique," Belle said.

Ava and Trina bent over the plants on the forest floor and quickly snapped a few holo-images. Brill and Pavish picked up pebbles and started throwing them at each other.

A short time later, Lucas stood up and looked around. "Can anybody see Ms. Polley?"

Belle looked around. She couldn't.

"Ms. Polley!" Brill called out.

She didn't reply.

"Come on," Lucas said. "Let's catch up to her. I'm sure she went straight up this way."

"She did say she was just heading up the path a little way," Belle agreed.

They shoved their water bottles back into their packs and followed Lucas up the path. Belle forgot her tiredness for a moment. She did not want to get lost in this forest. But surely, if they couldn't find their teacher, they could just follow the path back down to their campsite. Right?

Sol 48, Autumn/Cycle 106

We've been walking this path for ages with no sign of our teacher. We're taking a break — again — because Ava's been crying. I keep thinking about Ms. Polley. Has she even noticed that we're gone?

We came to a fork in the path earlier. Ta'al said she could see Ms. Polley's footprints, so we took the left path. But they could be anyone's prints. We can't be the only people on this trail, right?

The sun is beginning to set and it's getting colder. We've shouted for help and tried to contact Melody at the campsite. But nothing seems to work. I'm trying my best not to panic. I think we're LOST!

CHAPTER THREE
:LOST:

"We should turn back," Belle suggested, after they'd walked for what seemed like forever. "Ms. Polley might have taken the other path."

"We didn't see any footprints on that path, and the plants hadn't been trampled on," Ta'al said. "I don't think anyone has been on that path for several days, at least."

Ava let out a loud wail. "I just want to get back to the campsite and have a warm meal. I'm so hungry."

31

Belle wanted to say they should've turned back ages ago. But she didn't want to sound whiny like Ava or appear to agree with her. However, she had to admit to herself that Ava was right.

"You may be right," Bell said to Ta'al. "But it'll be getting dark soon. I think we should head back."

Exhausted and slightly panicked, the class moved quietly down the trail. Belle thought that walking downhill would be easier, but she had to pay more attention to things she could trip over. And the light was growing dimmer with each passing minute.

They arrived back at the fork in the path and took a right.

"Wait!" Brill called. "Did anyone notice this other path on our way up?

They looked back at the trail. There were actually three possible paths to take. They hadn't noticed the last one on the way up.

"This is the way we came," Pavish said, indicating the path they were on.

"No, this is," Lucas said, pointing to the path on their left.

"Look, there's a sign on the ground," Trina said. "It looks like it got knocked over by accident."

Brill and Lucas cleaned off the old sign and lifted it back up. It had an arrow pointing toward the third path. It read, "Exit."

"I told you. We should go this way," Lucas said.

"I'm with Pavish on this," Belle said. "We came up that way."

"How did we miss all the paths before?" Ava whined.

"I think Belle is right," Ta'al said.

"Of course you do," Ava said. "You two never disagree."

"And you might both be wrong," Trina said.

Belle couldn't believe they were arguing. She was positive that she was right. But Trina and Lucas were sure that they were right. As they argued, the sun was dropping lower in the sky. Soon it would be pitch black on the mountain, and then what would they do?

"Fine, we'll go your way." Belle finally decided it was best not to fight over this. They could get to the bottom and then see who was right. The main thing right now was to get off the trail and back to the campground.

Lucas led the way this time. They walked in silence. Once in a while, someone would say they didn't know how Ms. Polley could lose a group of seven students. No one wanted to admit how scared they were. But Belle could hear it in their voices.

After several minutes, Belle felt something cold and wet on her arm.

"It's starting to rain," she said, dismayed.

They all stopped and looked up.

"Maybe it's just moisture from the leaves," Ta'al said.

"Nope, I felt two drops on my face," Lucas said.

And then it began to drizzle. Everyone pulled their raincoats out of their bags, slipped them on, and pressed the buttons on the sleeves. The coats sealed themselves to the student's bodies, acting like a second skin. They continued on their trek.

A little while later Belle was so focused on not tripping that she didn't realize that the sun had almost set. When she looked up, she saw only thin slivers of light piercing through the treetops like golden threads. Soon nobody would be able to see where they were going.

"We should've reached the bottom by now," Ta'al said. "Maybe we took the wrong path."

"Any path that heads downward should get us to level ground, right?" Lucas said.

"I'm shivering," Ava complained. "It's so cold."

"Maybe we should just stay here and let Ms. Polley and Melody come find us," Belle said. "We could be getting deeper into the forest for all we know."

At this point, nobody wanted to argue anymore. They each picked a spot and sat down. Some took a sip of water from their bottles. Brill pulled out a snack he'd brought and began munching it noisily.

"I'm hungry," Ava said, rummaging through her bag for supplies. "And this rain is getting heavier."

Belle looked at her coat sleeve. It was covered with a film of water. She could almost feel the cold rain soak through her coat and onto her skin.

"We should look for some shelter," she said. She was trying not to sound as scared as she felt. She knew there would be no point in panicking. Melody would notice how long they'd been gone. Belle knew her android would find them. She always came through.

Nobody moved, so Belle and Ta'al went exploring. Luckily, although their comm devices weren't getting any reception in the forest, they worked well as flashlights. Using their backpacks as shields against prickly plants, they pushed aside anything that could be hiding a cave. After several tries, Ta'al found a shallow cave that could fit the entire group. It was small, but enough to let them stay out of the rain.

Ta'al went to fetch the rest of the class. Meanwhile Belle removed vines and sticks to clean up the cave floor.

She shoved aside some of the plants that coated the cave walls. In one spot she found no wall behind the plants. The cave went deeper than she'd thought. Peering into the darkness, she shivered. It reminded her too much of a hole she's fallen through earlier that summer.

"Let's put all our food together," Lucas instructed everyone after they had arrived and settled inside the cave. "We should share and ration what we have, just in case we're here for a while."

The seven classmates emptied their backpacks and took note of what they had. There were several snack bars, seven half-empty bottles of water, seven comm devices with no reception, and a first aid kit. There was also a length of rope that Ta'al had packed.

"You never know when rope will come in useful," she said, sitting the farthest inside the small cave. "If someone falls down a cliff, for example."

This time it was Brill that wailed. He was scared now, and he didn't care that everyone knew it. Also, he'd eaten most of his snack and was still hungry.

"I want to go home," he cried.

"Don't be such a baby," Trina nudged him. She handed him one of the snack bars. "At least we're safe from the rain."

"I'm going to put two of our devices on flashlight mode," Lucas said, standing back up. "I'll leave them outside the cave on the path, in case anyone comes looking for us."

"Good idea," Belle said. "I'm sure Melody is looking for us as we speak." She pressed the button on her coat sleeve, releasing the seal. The rain coat now acted like a regular coat, and she felt less suffocated. She leaned back against the thick vine wall and breathed slowly.

Around her, she heard sniffles and sighs.

"This cave goes pretty far in," Belle told the group. She figured if they could distract themselves for a while, they wouldn't be so scared. And time would move faster. "Anyone feel like exploring?"

Nobody replied. They were mostly looking at their food supply or at their own feet. Only Ta'al looked at her, giving her a weak smile.

"Did I ever tell you what it was like when I fell into that cave last summer?" Belle needed for them to feel optimistic. If they all just sat there, she would start to panic. "You know — in the Barren Lands? That cave is a museum now. It celebrates the Sulux-Nabian alliance."

"We know that," Pavish said, sounding annoyed. "It was all over the news, and we've all been there."

Belle ignored his tone. "Yes, but in the beginning it was just me, all alone in the dark — a lot like this. We're kind of lucky that we're all here together."

"Lucky?" Trina said, surprised.

"Being alone in that shaft was scary," Belle said. "But when I heard Ta'al's voice, and later Melody's, I felt better. I wasn't alone."

Heads nodded in agreement. Slowly, everyone began to pay attention to Belle's story. She continued speaking, telling them of how she explored the hole she'd fallen into. She shared how she discovered that it was a giant cave, which turned out to be an ancient site full of artifacts.

"Maybe we can explore this cave," she said, lighting up her comm device. "Who knows what might be in here?"

This idea seemed to brighten the others' moods. They grabbed flashlights and Belle showed them where she'd found the entrance to the rest of the cave. The hole wasn't very big. They had to lower their heads to enter. They held hands to stay together and some shared lights. Belle and Ta'al led the group, keeping their hands out in front.

The cave ceiling disappeared after a few steps, revealing a larger cave. It wasn't as big as the one Belle had fallen into before, but it was big enough that they could all stand comfortably. They shined their lights along the walls and floor. It was dusty inside, filled with pebbles and rocks, but very little vegetation.

"The sunlight must not get in this far," Ta'al said. "That explains why there aren't any plants here."

"This would make a good place for an animal to hibernate in," Lucas said.

"Hello!" Belle called out to make sure nothing else was in the cave. She didn't want to think about what kind of animal would use this place as its home.

"Let's each look for a rock or pebble or something," she suggested. "We could log it and add it to our geology study."

Ava groaned. "Even without the teacher here, we're still doing school work. Unbelievable!" But she didn't argue further. In fact she and Trina quickly became engrossed in finding the most perfect stone.

Belle and Ta'al searched the farthest inside the cave. As Belle ran her hand along the cave wall, she thought she saw a sparkle of light.

"Look over here," she said to Ta'al, pointing toward the cave wall. "Shine your light there."

Ta'al did as Belle asked. As she swept her light over the wall, something caught Belle's eye. The spot that Ta'al had just illuminated was now shining. It was as if the stone wall had absorbed the light and now reflected it back.

"Look at this!" Belle called her friends over. She shined her light on a spot on the cave wall for a few seconds and then moved the light away. She blinked several times. One by one, tiny specks of light began to twinkle in the wall. Everyone gasped.

"Is this bio-luminescence?" Ta'al asked.

"I don't know." Belle thought it was a beautiful sight, like the sky on a starry night.

"No," Lucas said. "Bio-luminescence is when living creatures give off light on their own. These rocks aren't alive."

"Or *are* they? Ooooohhh," Brill and Pavish said at the same time, making silly spooky noises. Belle was glad they were getting over their fear. But she didn't appreciate them giving her more things to be afraid of.

"These rocks must contain fluorescent minerals," Lucas explained, "just like glow rocks."

"Cool!" everyone said.

"I wonder if we can dig some out and take them with us?" Trina said.

"They'd make really pretty night lights," Ava added.

"We're not supposed to remove anything from nature, remember?" Belle reminded everyone of what Ms. Polley had told them.

"One little one won't hurt," Brill said.

"I suppose so," Belle said doubtfully.

Everyone got to work, trying to dig out a rock. Pavish found some glowing rocks on the ground too, so he crouched down to dig those out. Belle and Ta'al moved to another wall and tried to feel for any loose rocks that they might take with them.

"There's one right here, at the very bottom of this back wall." Belle squatted on her heels. With the tips of her fingers, she found a small rock that was coming loose. She had to stretch to pull it off. She balanced on her tip-toes and leaned over. She was just about to pull the stone loose when she lost her balance and fell over.

The ground beneath her gave way suddenly, and Belle rolled down a dark slope. Over and over she went, farther into the cave. She heard screams and knew they weren't her own. She was too stunned to scream. All she could think was — *Not again!*

CHAPTER FOUR
⋮POISONED⋮

Belle leaned against the cave wall as Ta'al and Ava
did their best to clean the gash on her leg. The fall hadn't
been as far as Belle had thought. But it resulted in a deep
cut on her shin. The pain was terrible.

"It's lucky you brought the first-aid kit, Ava," Ta'al
said, using a sterilizing spray on Belle's leg.

Belle shrieked. "Agh! That made it worse! My skin is burning." Ta'al ignored her.

"Our parents taught us to always have a kit with us, just in case." Ava beamed with pride. She pulled out a roll of white bandage and got ready to wrap Belle's leg.

Belle's head pounded as her friends gathered closely around her to stare at her injury. She tried not to watch what Ta'al and Ava were doing. Soon, she felt the tightness of the bandage wrapped around her lower leg. The pain lessened to a dull throbbing.

"I'm going outside," Lucas said, looking a bit sick. "In case anyone is looking for us. Maybe I'll find a spot where the comm device works."

"Don't go too far," Belle warned. "We don't want to lose you."

Lucas ducked out of the cave. The others gathered near Belle to look at their rock collection. They "oohed" and "aahed," flashing their lights on the stones and watching them glow.

Time soon seemed to slow down for Belle. Her head felt fuzzy. Strange halos surrounded her friends' heads, and their voices sounded slow and strange. The throbbing in her leg died down, but now there was a new and strange sensation. It was as if tiny worms were crawling through her skin and up into her thigh. It tickled, but in a painful way. The feeling made Belle squirm. She rubbed her leg, trying to push the wormy sensation away.

She swept her hand across her forehead. Her face and hair were wet with sweat. And it was getting harder to breathe.

"Ta'al," she called, sounding weak. "Did someone close the door to the cave?"

Ta'al came to her side. She put her hand on Belle's face and mumbled some Nabian words Belle hadn't heard before. "*Svo tenya reyal* — you don't look right," she said.

"What does that mean?" Belle said. She found it hard to focus on her friend's face. She blinked several times.

"Everyone?" Ta'al turned to the others. "I think Belle is getting worse."

Belle couldn't make out her friends' words anymore. She knew they were crowding around her and talking very loudly. But she didn't understand what they were saying. She licked her lips.

"She wants water," she heard someone say. And then a bottle was at her lips. She sipped some water, but it tasted funny — as if the water was taken straight from the stream. She spat it back out.

"No!" she heard Ta'al's voice.

There were more words she couldn't understand. She tried to speak, but she couldn't remember what she wanted to say. She felt very confused.

A sudden, sharp pain crossed her cheek, and Belle was alert again.

"Did you slap me?" she said, to no one in particular.

"Belle, you need to stay awake," Ava said, towering over her. "I heard that it's the best thing to do."

"What's wrong?" she asked. She knew it couldn't be good. Something strange was happening to her, and it was beginning to frighten her.

"Calm down," Ta'al said. "Just breathe slowly."

Belle hadn't realized that her breathing had become quick and shallow. It made her feel dizzy.

"Lucas and Pavish went to find help," Ta'al continued, putting a bottle to Belle's lips. "You're going to be *melyanti*, I mean . . . fine."

Ta'al didn't sound very convincing. Belle took a few more sips. The water still tasted disgusting. She heard Trina and Ava crying softly. She knew she was in trouble.

Something hard and cold slipped under Belle's body. Her friends' crying turned into squeals. What was happening? Something else must have been in the cave with them, and it was now coming out to get them!

And then a very familiar voice spoke into Belle's ear.

"I have you. You are safe now." It was Melody!

"Something in this part of the mountain is blocking the signals from our comm devices," Melody said as she led the others away from the cave. "I have tried to scan for it, but I cannot get a reading."

Belle blinked hard and her android friend's face came into focus. She was in Melody's arms, and they were walking downhill. The shrieks she'd heard before turned out to be cries of happiness and relief. They were saved!

"Belle, your injury looks bad," Melody said. "We are taking you straight to the nearest medical facility. It is on the outskirts of Pettit. It will take a while."

Belle nodded. Or at least, she thought she nodded. She couldn't be sure. Everything around her swirled in streaks of dull color. It felt like her ears were filling up with shoat wool, and it grew harder and harder to keep her eyes open. After a while, Belle gave up trying, and the whole world went black.

● ● ● ●

When Belle awoke, she found herself in a very comfortable bed. But her arms itched. She reached over to scratch, and her skin pulled.

"Ouch!" Belle exclaimed.

"Do not try to move," Melody said. "You are in a medical facility. You are safe."

Belle squeezed her eyes shut and reopened them. Bit by bit, she took notice of her surroundings. She was in a small room with medical androids on both sides of her bed. Tubes ran from them to her arms. A machine overhead projected a holo-image, showing information about her body and what was happening to her. Her room had a window on one side that showed the outside world. On the other side was another window that looked out to the rest of the facility. Several faces were pushed up against it. Her friends were watching. Even Ms. Polley stood with them. They all looked worried.

"Why . . ." Belle tried to speak, but her throat was dry and scratchy. It made speaking difficult.

Melody gave her glass with a straw. "You need to be hydrated," she said.

Belle took several large gulps of water. She hadn't realized how thirsty she was. Then she spluttered and coughed because she drank too quickly.

"Why don't they come inside?" she tried again. She waved weakly at her friends.

"You are being kept in isolation for now," Melody said. "The doctors are unsure what caused your infection, and they did not want to take any risks. I am not vulnerable to infection. I am the only one allowed in here."

"Am I really that sick?" Belle tried to give her friends a brave smile. Ta'al was signaling something with her hands, but Belle didn't understand it.

"Your parents have been informed. They are preparing to come here."

"No," Belle said, turning to her android. "It's just a cut. I'll be better in no time. I want to finish this camping trip."

"We are awaiting one final lab report," Melody said, refilling Belle's cup with water. "Your friends showed me the rocks you found. I was unable to analyze them, but I suspect that something in them caused an infection. The doctors are waiting for a full analysis of your blood. Once we have that, your parents will decide if they should come."

Belle breathed a sigh of relief. She didn't want her first trip without her parents to end so quickly. She could kick herself for being so careless. She had to get better soon. She didn't want to ruin the camping trip for her whole class.

"When will the report be ready?" she asked.

Before Melody could answer, the door to her room slid open. A woman walked in, covered from head to toe in what looked like a space suit. Belle could only see her face through a clear window in her headpiece. She had a grim

expression on her face. Belle's heart dropped. Was this the end of camping for her?

"You have your android to thank," she said. "We were using a completely different treatment when she told us about the rocks you were exposed to."

Exposed to? That sounded like a bad thing.

"Why aren't my friends affected?" Belle asked. "They were near the rocks too."

"When you cut yourself, small traces of the rock entered your blood stream. These are highly unusual rocks." The doctor tapped a few buttons on her datapad to project Belle's test results on the holo-screen above her. Melody was very interested in the results.

"We found traces of iron, gold, and . . ." the doctor frowned strangely. "Fluinium."

"Fluinium?" Belle repeated. She was more interested in the gold in her blood. She'd never heard of Fluinium.

"Fascinating," Melody said, studying the report closely. "Fluinium does not occur naturally on Mars."

"Not that we know of," the doctor said.

"So, it came from somewhere off Mars?" Belle tried to read the report herself, but it made her head hurt.

"Fluinium is a very rare and valuable element. It exists on only one in three-hundred-thousand asteroids in the

Asteroid Belt," Melody explained. "It was only discovered in the last fifty cycles. It is used, among other things, to power the engines of advanced starships. The technology is still experimental, but it could mean the beginning of interstellar travel for humans. Everyone is keeping their eye on the development of Fluinium-powered engines. It is the next big thing."

It took several minutes for Belle to fully understand what Melody had said.

"So, you're saying I have a precious metal in my blood, and that it's making me sick?" she asked.

The doctor nodded, which made her suit crinkle loudly. "There are a few rare reports of asteroid miners having symptoms similar to yours, after exposure to Fluinium. We believe the element is poisonous to humans if it gets into the bloodstream."

"I've been poisoned?" Belle understood that perfectly. "Am I going to die?"

"As I told you, Belle," Melody said quickly. "You are safe." She pointed to the report above Belle. "Now that we know that Fluinium made you ill, the doctors will be able to treat you."

"Yes," the doctor said. "Doctors in Utopia have experience treating Fluinium poisoning. They're sending us the formula for the antidote as we speak. We'll duplicate it in our labs. You should be well enough to go home by the end of the day."

The doctor patted Belle on the arm with her gloved hand. As she exited the room, she waved Belle's friends to come in.

"There's no danger, now that we know what her condition is," the doctor said.

Ms. Polley and the entire class filed into Belle's room.

"I'm so sorry I've ruined the camping trip," Belle said to her friends.

"Are you kidding?" Brill blurted out. "This is the most exciting thing ever. And there's a cafeteria here!"

"It beats being stuck in a cave in the rain." Lucas grinned and squeezed Belle's hand. He looked so happy to see her. It made Belle blush.

"I've informed your parents," Ms. Polley said. She looked extremely tired. "All the parents, actually. They're deciding on what we should do next."

"Oh please, let us stay!" Belle begged. "The doctor says I'll be out of here soon. We still have another three nights on our trip. I promise I'll be extra good."

Ms. Polley looked at her class. Everyone pleaded with her to let them stay. Finally, she surrendered.

"I'm the one who's sorry for losing you lot," she said. Her dark eyes were shiny. "I was so focused on finding a comm signal, that I didn't notice a root sticking out of the ground. I tripped and badly twisted my ankle. By the time I managed to hobble back, you had all left. You were supposed to stay put."

She grimaced, looking guilty. "But I can't blame you for coming to look for me. You must have been scared. When I saw you were gone, I limped back to the area with a signal and called for Melody's help."

"Yes, that is how we were able to locate you so quickly." Melody held out another cup of water for Belle to sip.

"Quickly?" Ta'al said, helping to put the straw in Belle's mouth. "We were in that cave for a long time."

"You were missing for precisely one and one half hours." Melody said. "Did it feel longer to you?"

Everyone nodded, and then began talking at the same time. They each described their own feelings and thoughts about their experience. It was a good sound to Belle. She could finally hear and understand them clearly. Her body must be recovering even before getting the antidote.

The medical android attached to her right arm beeped several times. Everyone stopped talking to look at it. Melody checked the readings it was giving out.

"The droid is dispensing some medicines to help keep you well until the antidote is ready," Melody explained

Ms. Polley clapped. "I'm so relieved you'll be okay, Belle. I'll update your parents." She headed for the door.

As she opened the door to Belle's room, two large Martian humans were standing outside. With them were two Protectors, standing tall and silent. The Martians were speaking to the doctor, who was no longer in her protective suit. She was shaking her head and clutching her datapad to her chest. As Ms. Polley emerged from the room, the Martians tried to enter.

"We would like to speak to the children involved in the incident," the shorter man said.

Children? Belle didn't like being referred to as a child. They were all thirteen and fourteen already. They weren't children. But the Martians were a little too scary to argue with. So she kept quiet.

Melody moved to stand between Belle, her friends, and the door. "You are required to have parental permission to interact with these young people." She cited the regulations to the Martians.

"We are BAMCorp representatives," the taller lady Martian huffed. "We have the authority to speak to anyone exposed to any of our material."

"What material is that?" Ms. Polley said. "My students haven't been anywhere near the Corporation's property. There's none here in Pettit."

The lady Martian pulled out her datapad and showed Ms. Polley a chart of some kind. "BAMCorp has exclusive rights to all traces of Fluinium."

Belle looked at Melody, confused.

"The Belt Asteroid Mining Corporation owns Fluinium," Melody explained.

"So, they want me to return the stuff that's in my blood?"

Sol 48, Autumn/Cycle 106
Almost midnight.

The doctor brought the antidote just now. I can already feel it working. She said I should stay the night in the hospital. I didn't mind the comfier bed, but I was sad not to join my friends back at the campsite. Ms. Polley promised to be here for me first thing tomorrow morning. I feel fine. Melody hasn't stopped making me drink water. If the antidote doesn't work, I'm sure I've flushed all the poison out with all this water already!

CHAPTER FIVE
:PROTECTING:
THE PLANET

"I'm fine, really I am!" Belle said to the holo-image of her parents. They still looked worried even though Belle was on her feet and twirling around. Facing them again, she put her hands together and pleaded for them to let her stay.

Yun puckered his lips and frowned.

"Only if you promise to let Melody take your vital signs every morning and send them to us," Zara gave in. She lifted Thea into her arms so Belle could wave goodbye to her sister.

Belle walked out of the medical facility feeling much stronger. It was hard to believe she'd been so sick only a day ago. Melody kept reminding her to take it slow. But she felt full of energy, much like her dog Raider when he was let out of the stable each morning. Her teacher and classmates were waiting for her and Melody nearby in the hover-wagon. They were happy to see her. Even Pavish and Brill gave her a hug — which never happened. Lucas was the last to hug her.

"I'm so glad you're all right," he said, his light purple face turning a little red.

"Th-thanks." Belle's voice sounded funny. She had goose-bumps and her heart skipped a beat. She didn't understand why she was reacting this way. For a moment she worried that some poison might still be in her system.

The trip back to the campsite went by quickly. Belle couldn't wait to sit around their fire and tell stories, while Melody made everyone something delicious to eat. She'd had only one meal at the medical facility, and it had been tasteless. She badly wanted Melody's cooking.

"What's going on here?" Ms. Polley said as they pulled up at the campground's entrance.

"There are so many people!" Ta'al exclaimed, peeking out the windows.

All the students pressed their faces against the windows. Lines of people — humans and aliens, were heading into the campground. They had to stop at the small hut out front to register before entering.

"I guess it's a holiday or something," Belle said. "Looks like we'll have neighbors now."

After parking the wagon in their spot, Belle and her friends hopped off and found more people walking through their campsite. Some of the people were carrying holo-signs down by their sides. Others had made physical signs out of sticks and boards. Several signs were painted with words that Belle couldn't quite make out. What was most unusual about the people is that no one spoke. They just walked quietly past the campsite.

"What's happening?" Ta'al asked no one in particular.

"Let's find out," Belle said. She walked up to one of the people, a Sulux, and asked him why he was here.

"We have to stop the Corporation," he said. The ridges on his arms and face were sharp and shiny in the bright morning light, making him appear as if he was ready for a fight. "They can't destroy our land."

Belle wanted to ask more questions, but the man just kept walking. She was about to stop another person when Ms. Polley clapped her hands to get the students' attention.

"We're going to visit the museum this morning," she announced. "It's not far, within walking distance. Seal your tents so that your belongings will stay safe."

Belle heard Trina and Ava groan at the word museum, but this time she wasn't annoyed at them. After being in a medical facility for a whole day, she'd missed the silliness of her friends.

The museum was a short distance from the hiking trail entrance. It wasn't a large building, but it was an interesting shape. It had a round dome in the middle, with straight armlike sections coming out from it. A transparent ring connected the outer ends of the arms. The structure looked similar to a solar-cycle wheel with six spokes. The entire building blended in with the mountain behind it. Belle imagined that from the sky, this building would be hard to spot.

Ms. Polley led them through one of the arm sections into the main dome. On the ceiling and along the walls was a holo-projection of the surrounding forest. Light beams pierced through the tree leaves and branches. There was even an occasional drip of water from above. It was holo-tech, so Belle saw the drops come down, but she didn't actually get wet. The scene made her think of her experience in the cave the day before. She shivered.

A lovely Nabian woman emerged from behind a door in front of them. She seemed to glide over to them. Nabians were very graceful on their feet. It often seemed as if they almost floated above the ground.

"I am Ju'arn, your guide for today." She spoke with a sing-song tone, and her eyes reflected the colors of the forest scene in the dome. "I am one of the curators here at the museum. I am happy to show you around."

Belle liked her immediately. And from the looks on her friends' faces, so did they.

Ju'arn led the way through the many exhibits. They began in the section featuring the plants and animals that lived in the forests around Mars' big volcanoes.

"Olympus is the biggest mountain," said Ju'arn. "But Mars has many volcanoes. I am sure you are familiar with the three closer to where you live — Mount Arsia, Mount Pavonis, and Mount Ascreus. Martians have kept their original names from when Terrans first discovered them. Sulux and Nabian technology was used to terraform the land around these volcanoes. Today these areas are maintained as forests, to be preserved forever."

Ju'arn showed them a holo-vid of how the terraforming process was done. The real process took more than one hundred cycles, but in the vid, it took only a few minutes. Belle was fascinated as she watched the barren, red land change into lush green forests and rivers flowing from the mountains into large lakes.

"Scientists determined that the volcanoes were extinct by the time Mars was colonized," Ju'arn continued. "So when terraforming was completed, the mountains were turned into reservoirs, and a water cycle was created. This ensures that Mars will always have water."

"But the water is salty," Belle said.

Ju'arn looked pleased that Belle had paid attention. "Yes, that is true," she said, moving over to the next exhibit. It held a series of miniatures showing the various desalination plants all around the planet. Each building had a different design. "Mars' bedrock has many chemical elements that make the water undrinkable for humans. However, some alien species are able to survive on the water in its natural state. This is why we chose to use desalination plants. Terraforming underground would have been too destructive for the planet, and it would have excluded the needs of several Martian species. This was the most inclusive, environmentally-friendly option."

"So, no one would be left without water," Ta'al added. "Nabians can survive on any form of water. But I know Parsiv people need the minerals in the salt water."

"*Sia toh follari*," Ju'arn said, using the Nabian phrase for "that's right." She twirled her hands in a dance-like movement. It was a special Nabian greeting, just for Ta'al.

Ta'al beamed.

Ju'arn led the class to the next section that displayed the Martian water cycle, created to make the planet livable.

"Terraforming this region with a semi-tropical climate was very deliberate. We can make it rain here more often," she said, showing them the exhibit about weather patterns on Mars. "Believe it or not, it rarely snows on the ground in this region, even in winter. Only the higher elevations on the mountain get snow."

"Whoa!" Lucas said. "That's cool, except that we'd have school all year round."

Ju'arn smiled broadly. Then she explained how every part of the system had to be carefully balanced.

"If one part of a river became polluted, it would affect our water system all the way down the line," she said. "It is a very delicate system, even though the land seems to have a surprising ability to heal itself. Still, if any drastic changes were to happen, the whole system could collapse."

"What sort of thing would be considered drastic?" Ms. Polley asked, looking sideways at the class. Belle knew this meant they should pay attention.

Ju'arn swished her hand over a holo-display. It played through several scenarios. The first was a massive planet-wide quake. Next, one of the volcanoes erupted. In both scenes, the rivers and reservoirs were destroyed. Only a few of the desalination plants remained intact.

"These events are quite unlikely to happen," Ju'arn said. "However, this next possibility is more likely."

She swished her arm over the display again. This time, it showed the farms and towns around the mountains and rivers. Over a few seconds, the number of towns and farms grew — more and more people were added. The number of roads, transports, and buildings grew quickly.

"Look at the water!" Ava cried, pointing to the display.

"It's changing color," Lucas said. "Is that because of the growth of the towns?"

Ju'arn nodded. "As Martians, we must carefully monitor our growth in population and industry to keep it in balance with the planet's environment. As you know, over-population and industrial pollution brought about Earth's current sad condition. And we have all seen how people were forced to leave that planet."

"But Earth will heal, right?" Belle was hopeful. Her teacher on Earth had said the planet could heal itself, if Terrans allowed it to. But that it would take a long time.

"Given the chance, we believe it is possible," Ju'arn said. "For now, even our alien technology can do little to help restore Earth's natural beauty. But we must learn from those mistakes and ensure that Mars does not face the same problems. We must take care of our home."

Everyone nodded, feeling the gravity of Ju'arn's plea.

As the group headed back to the main dome, they heard voices. Many voices. Some of the people holding signs they had seen at the campground had come into the museum. It sounded as if they were all speaking at once.

"Please wait here," Ju'arn said. Her eyes changed color to dark brown. Belle knew it meant something was wrong.

Ta'al's eye color changed to match Ju'arn's. Belle put an arm around her best friend.

"I'm sure it's nothing," she said. "Probably too many people wanting to visit the museum at once."

"I'll go and see what's happening," Ms. Polley said, after several minutes of waiting. "Promise me you'll all stay right here."

They promised, but Ms. Polley was unsure. She made Melody promise instead, to make sure no one moved from this spot.

Watching from afar, Belle could see that Ju'arn and another museum official were upset with the new visitors.

On both sides, people were gesturing as if they were arguing. Belle grew curious. She slowly inched a little closer.

"Not too far," warned Melody.

"I just want to lean on this pillar," she replied. Melody allowed her to. Ta'al moved next to Belle as well. They were both trying to listen in on the conversations.

With a better view, Belle saw that the museum officials weren't speaking to the people with signs. Those people had followed and were crowding around the two Martians — the same ones who had visited Belle at the medical facility!

"Those are the BAMCorp representatives," Belle whispered to Ta'al.

"What are they doing here?" she asked.

Belle inched her way to the other side of the pillar and strained her ears to listen. She caught a few words. Fluinium was one of them.

"I think the BAMCorp people are trying to find out about the Fluinium we found," Belle said to Ta'al.

"So they'll want access to the cave," Ta'al said. "I wonder why the curators won't let them?"

Belle thought about that. BAMCorp was the biggest corporation on Mars. The capital city of Utopia was practically built by the company. Their business was to mine the asteroid belt between Mars and Jupiter. Belle's parents had originally moved to Mars to work for BAMCorp, but they had lost their jobs even before they started. Belle had never liked BAMCorp, but she knew they did important work. A lot of the minerals and precious metals used on Mars were mined by BAMCorp.

"Remember what Melody said about Fluinium?" Belle whispered to Ta'al.

"She said it's very rare and experimental," Ta'al said. "And that it's poisonous."

Belle did not need to be reminded of that. "I think they want the Fluinium in the cave."

"They have plenty in the asteroid belt," Ta'al replied. "Why would they need the tiny amount in the cave?"

Belle listened harder but couldn't hear much more. The curators looked angry. But the BAMCorp representatives were smug, as if they knew they'd win this argument. Ju'arn bowed out of the conversation and headed back toward Belle's group. Ms. Polley appeared beside her and they spoke in low tones until they reached Belle and her classmates.

"It looks like that's the end of our tour for today," Ms. Polley said. She looked a little pale and definitely upset about something.

The class protested. Everyone was enjoying the museum and clearly wanted to stay.

"Perhaps when all this is settled, you may return," Ju'arn said. Before Belle could ask her why they cut the tour short, their guide gave them the Nabian farewell sign and left.

On the way out, Belle and Ta'al asked Ms. Polley about what they'd overheard.

"You shouldn't have been eavesdropping," their teacher said. "And we may have to cut our camping trip short if things get too heated here."

"What's going on?" Belle asked.

Ms. Polley didn't need to answer. As the class turned the corner to head back to their campsite, a crowd of people was heading toward them. Many carried signs, and this time, held them high over their heads.

Down with BAMCorp!

Save our Water!

Leave our Forests Alone!

No Mining in Paradise.

As Belle read the signs, she realized what was happening and why the crowd had gathered.

"BAMCorp wants the Fluinium in that cave," she told her friends. "I'm sure they'll want to mine the volcano. But that seems risky. It could destroy the delicate balance of the whole environment."

Sol 49, Autumn/Cycle 106

Sitting in our tent, I can hear the voices of more people arriving to protest the mining of the cave. Ms. Polley was surprised at how quickly the protest was organized. News about the Fluinium find must have spread fast.

It's so beautiful here. I don't like the idea of BAMCorp mining here and ruining everything. I hope they know what they're doing. They have smart people working for them, right?

I've never seen a protest in real life. It might be fun. But it could be kind of scary.

CHAPTER SIX
:PROTEST!:

Melody served up a delicious meal that evening. Brill, Pavish, and Trina dug in as if they hadn't eaten in days. Ava picked at her food. Lucas, Ta'al, and Belle couldn't stop staring at the people as they walked past their site.

"Look at that sign," Lucas said, pointing to a holo-sign that read, *We Destroyed Earth. Don't Destroy Mars.*

"Do you think it might be dangerous for BAMCorp to mine the mountain?" Belle asked. "Surely they could do it safely. What about Nabian technology?"

Ta'al shrugged. "I don't know much about mining," she said. "It's not something Nabians have been involved with in the past."

"Maybe we should follow the protestors to see where they end up." Belle's eyes brightened at her own idea. She could barely eat with all the excitement that was building up around them.

"I object to that," Melody said, looking at Belle's untouched dinner. "Especially if you are not eating."

"I agree," Ms. Polley said. She emerged from her tent in time to hear their conversation. "I've been talking to your parents. They're anxious for us to return home."

"Please, can we just see where they're going?" Belle pleaded. "We won't get involved."

"Yeah!" Lucas jumped to his feet, ready to go. "At the very most, we'll ask them a few questions."

"It could be very educational," Ta'al added. She knew Ms. Polley wouldn't be able to resist that argument.

Ms. Polley shook her head and sighed. "I've checked the schedule and the next shuttle home is tomorrow morning. I thought we'd spend tonight at a motel in town."

Belle didn't want to stay in a motel. "Do we have to?" she asked. "We came here to camp out. And I haven't even gotten to sleep in my tent yet."

"What if we vote on it?" she pressed on, looking at her friends. "If everything stays peaceful, couldn't we stay the night here and leave first thing tomorrow?"

Brill and Pavish nodded at Belle, their mouths too full of food to speak. Lucas, Ta'al, and Trina also agreed with Belle. Ava was the only one who wanted to leave.

Belle volunteered to check out the protest. "I'll take Melody, and she can see if it's too dangerous to stay."

Seeing that her students had made up their minds, Ms. Polley reluctantly agreed. Lucas and Ta'al volunteered to go with Belle and Melody. Meanwhile, Ms. Polley and the others would clean up their campsite, in case they had to leave that night.

Belle led the way and they soon caught up to the crowd. The protestors walked quietly along the path to the trail, holding up their signs as they went.

Are they going to hike up to the cave? Belle wondered.

But then the crowd turned and headed toward the museum. As they passed the trailhead, two young Martian men emerged from the forest. They wore scarves across their foreheads, and heavy-looking boots. Their shirts had the letters DoO on them.

"Hello. Can I ask . . . what does DoO stand for?" Belle asked the first man.

"Defenders of Olympus," he said. The red ring around his irises glowed in the evening light. He was a Martian-born human. "Are you joining us?"

"We're trying to find out what's going on," Lucas jumped in.

"Our teacher feels it's too dangerous for us to stay here tonight," Ta'al said.

The man laughed. "She might be right," he said. "We'll have to see what happens."

"Don't scare them, Seb," the second man said. He stuck his hand out to Belle. "I'm Munny. This is my partner, Seb. We run the DoO."

Belle shook their hands and introduced herself, her friends, and Melody.

"The more that join us, the better," Munny said.

"Can you tell us why you're protesting?" Belle asked as they joined the end of the line of people.

Seb pulled a mini-datapad out of his pocket and shook it. A holo-sign popped out, and he held it up high. It read, *Defenders of Olympus, We Protect Nature.*

"We think that BAMCorp already mines plenty of Fluinium from the asteroid belt," he said. "There's no need to come after the small amount in this area."

Someone in the crowd shouted something, and Seb and Munny both cheered.

"Why is there Fluinium here anyway?" Ta'al asked. "I read that it's extremely rare to find on a planet."

Munny looked impressed by Ta'al's question. "You're right," he said. "No one really knows, since Fluinium has never been discovered here before. Mars still has some secrets we don't know about."

"So, when we found Fluinium in the cave, it was like the discovery of the century!" Lucas' eyes grew wide.

Seb and Munny stopped to stare at them. "Wait a minute. You're those kids?"

"Belle was exposed and almost died from Fluinium poisoning!" Ta'al said.

Seb and Munny exclaimed so loudly that others turned to see what was going on. Munny repeated what Ta'al had said and got quite a reaction from the crowd. Belle blushed from all the attention.

"I tend to get into a lot of scrapes," she said. That made everyone laugh. Even Melody turned to nod her agreement.

"So, why is mining the Fluinium a bad thing?" Belle changed the subject so people wouldn't keep looking at her as if she were a miracle of science. "Can't they just take the Fluinium and leave?"

Munny grew quiet, as if she'd brought him back to reality. "It's not that simple. Finding Fluinium in that cave means that there's probably more of it deep inside the mountain. It may even be found throughout the region around the volcano. It could be in the bedrock or on the surface. No one knows."

"So they'd want to search everywhere?" Belle imagined people digging holes all over the forest.

Munny went on. "Exactly. Although mining technology has improved greatly since Earth days, there are still dangers."

"For one thing," Seb said. "Mining uses a lot of water. Sure, it gets recycled. But the runoff may be polluted. Toxins could poison the ground water."

"And those elements could be radioactive too," Munny said. "It could be even more poisonous than what you experienced, Belle."

Belle mouthed, *Wow*. Lucas was quiet, and Ta'al looked serious.

"It could be even worse," Seb said, waving his sign again. "BAMCorp would also have to build recycling and purifying plants to preserve the environment. But that would mean destroying at least part of the forest to make way for those buildings."

Munny waved his arm in an arc. "Much of this beautiful forest would be cut down. Only after they've sucked the area dry of Fluinium would they restore it. But it would be too late then."

"And mining uses a lot of power," Seb said. "That has to be taken from somewhere. Power for the company means a drain on power for everyone else nearby."

"Mining this mountain would be a great strain on both the land and the people in this region. We don't think the environment will survive the process." Munny took Seb's sign and held it out to Belle. "We'd essentially be turning the mountain over to BAMCorp to do with as they please."

Belle looked at the holo-sign and thought about what they'd said. Ju'arn had told her class about the delicate nature of Mars' environment. She'd made them promise to do their part to keep the planet strong and healthy. Seb and Munny's story backed up everything the guide had told them, as well as what Belle had guessed on her own.

"So, will you join us?" Munny said.

Belle smiled and took the sign. She held it as high as she could.

"Defenders of Olympus!" she shouted.

"Protect Mars!" Lucas joined in. Ta'al cheered with the crowd.

They were part of the protest now.

Sol 49, Autumn/Cycle 106

Lucas, Ta'al, and I are sitting with a group of protestors, showing our signs and making very little noise. The BAMCorp reps are inside the museum talking to the curators and the Mayor of Pettit. Someone said an official from Tharsis City is here too. But we can't be sure.

The protestors are worried about the future, but they also seem relaxed. Everyone is so friendly. They smile and wave at us. They're impressed that teenagers are interested in social issues. A couple of people even congratulated us.

Melody went back to the campsite to get us some water. I don't know what's taking her so long. But she promised to watch over us, so I'm sure she'll show up soon.

CHAPTER SEVEN
⫶MEET THE PRESS⫶

The late afternoon heat was starting to bother Belle. Melody was still nowhere to be seen, and she was carrying their water. Seb and Munny had left to try to get into the meeting with the BAMCorp representatives.

"I'll go see if I can get some water," Belle said. She stood up and stretched. Sitting still for so long was harder than she'd expected.

Ta'al and Lucas agreed to stay until she returned.

"If nothing happens soon, I'd rather go back to camp," Lucas said.

"*Caluk* — wait. Let's give it a few more minutes." Ta'al had her eyes and ears focused on the museum doors. "They're still negotiating." The doors were transparent, so the protestors could see the BAMCorp officials talking to the curators. They were huddled around the counter just inside the building. Their gestures and facial expressions kept everyone's attention, even if those outside couldn't hear anything.

"I'm going to see if I can find Melody, or some water," Belle told her friends.

She stepped through the crowds seated around the museum site. She walked through a large group of Martians and found herself on a path. It led up to the museum's front doors and was being kept clear of people by small droids.

"Where can I find some water?" Belle asked one droid. But she didn't hear its answer. At that moment, a series of black land transports pulled up at the end of the path. The transport doors opened and a bunch of people exited. The group included aliens and humans, and they were all dressed in stiff coats. They carried boxes and datapads, and they all looked very serious.

Scientists.

Belle recognized them. The coats were similar to those worn by the researchers who studied the ancient site she had discovered earlier that summer. The scientists strode up the path to the museum door. The last one in line was a petite alien woman. Belle didn't know the name of her species. She was about a foot shorter than Belle and had very pointed features. She also had insectlike wings on her shoulders, which didn't seem to help her fly. Belle couldn't decide what the wings could be for.

"Excuse me," Belle said to her. "Are you here to mine the Fluinium deposits?"

The scientist looked up from her datapad. Her bright yellow eyes glowered at Belle. She didn't reply, but she also stopped to look around. Her eyes widened to half the size of her face.

"Why are all these people here?" she asked.

"We're here to protect the mountain," Belle replied.

The scientist looked at Belle as if she hadn't seen her there before. Then her eyes came together, almost melding into one huge eyeball. She opened her mouth to speak. Belle braced herself to be yelled at. *After all, that's what happens to protestors, isn't it?*, she thought.

Just as the first words spilled from the scientist's mouth, another alien fluttered over. This one was a species Belle had met before. Most of her people were journalists. In fact, Belle had met this very one after discovering the ancient site. This alien had interviewed Belle at school. She recognized the alien's long green hair and sparkling wings that kept her in the air. She floated high enough to look down on Belle and the scientist. In her hands she carried a holo-cam and a datapad.

"Hello again," the journalist said to Belle. "We keep meeting in the most unexpected places."

"You remember me?" Belle asked.

"You're hard to forget," she said. "You seem to get into a lot of scrapes."

Belle laughed. She'd just said the same thing earlier.

"My name is Yixa," she said. "I'm Galerian. We are news gatherers, by nature and by profession."

"It's nice to meet you again, Yixa," Belle said.

The scientist stood between them, staring first at Belle and then at Yixa. "I shall not interrupt your reunion then," she said and moved along the path.

As she walked away, a BAMCorp official, the short one from the medical facility, came out to meet them.

"What's the press doing here?" he demanded. "Who invited you?"

"No one invites the press," Yixa said, readying her holo-cam. "We go where the news is." She pointed it at the rep. "Care to give a statement?"

The rep's face puffed up, and his ears went all red. He gestured to the scientist to move into the building. Yixa hovered upward to film the crowd of protestors.

"Looks like you've got trouble brewing," she said.

The BAMCorp rep fiddled with his earpiece. He mumbled something and then nodded several times.

"Wait," he said to Yixa. He was looking at Belle. "BAMCorp would like to show that we are not here to disrupt or destroy anything." His lips widened into an ugly smile. Belle could tell it was forced. "We have nothing to hide. In fact, we were just about to invite this young student to join our team of scientists at the cave where she discovered the Fluinium. We thought she would like to witness the analysis of the site. To further her education, of course."

The poor man sputtered his words, as if he were coming up with them as he spoke. By this point, his face

was so red and puffy that Belle was afraid he might burst. But Yixa seemed pleased by this suggestion.

"I'd like to follow Belle through this experience," Yixa said. "It will make for an interesting perspective."

"But of course," said the rep through his fake smile. "That's what we had planned for. It is most fortunate that you two met just as I was coming to get her. Ms. Song, you should follow Sasha here. She is the junior scientist on this expedition."

It took Belle a moment to understand what she was expected to do. "Can my friends come too?"

The rep waved his hands in the air, as if he was surrendering. "Oh, why not?" He pulled out a cloth and wiped his forehead. "The more the merrier. It'll be good for the Corporation's image. It'll show that we're not here to do any harm — just scientific research."

Yixa made a sound that was half snort, half laugh. She lowered herself, meeting Belle eye to eye.

"Go get your friends," she said, flapping her wings. "Then if you don't mind, I'd like you to show me where you found the precious mineral." She twisted around to the scientist and the rep. "We'll meet the rest of you on the mountain."

Belle headed back to Ta'al and Lucas. She told her friends what had happened.

"How do you always get caught up in the middle of things?" Ta'al asked. She looked troubled. "I think we should to back and tell Ms. Polley first, or at least wait for Melody to get back."

"There's no time." Lucas said. "We're getting front row seats to this show!"

Belle couldn't decide if she was excited or nervous. She had a sneaky feeling that she was being used. But her curiosity was too strong to ignore. Lucas was right. This was a chance to find out exactly what BAMCorp intended. She wasn't so thirsty anymore. And finding Melody could wait a bit longer.

CHAPTER EIGHT
:CONFRONTATIONS:

Belle felt strange entering the cave again. Even with the lights that Yixa shined into the cave, the place still made Belle shudder. She pressed her hands against the cave wall as she ducked her head to get inside. She didn't want to fall down and get scratched — or poisoned — again.

Yixa flew ahead and lit up a large section of the cave. Sasha, the junior scientist, followed behind. "Please, show me exactly where you fell," she said to Belle.

Yixa prepared her holo-cam. A bright red light came on. She had begun recording already.

Belle led Sasha to the back corner of the cave.

"Right here," she said, pointing. "Be careful, it's slippery."

Sasha put down her equipment and slipped on some thick gloves that went all the way up her arms. She already wore knee-high boots. Then she crouched down and got to work, carving out pieces of the rock face.

Belle, Ta'al, and Lucas found an out of the way boulder to sit on. Yixa came over and asked them about their experience in the cave. She prodded them for every detail.

When they were done sharing their story, Belle walked over to Sasha. The scientist was placing rock samples onto her special datapad to analyze them. She sat back against the cave wall to wait for the results.

"How do you think the Fluinium came to be here in this cave?" Belle asked, sitting beside Sasha.

Sasha shrugged. "It's possible that an asteroid crashed here millions of years ago."

"Really? Do you think it caused the volcano to form?" Belle said, picking up a loose rock to examine it.

"Maybe. This whole region may be one gigantic crater created by a huge asteroid," Sasha said. "Perhaps the volcano formed afterward."

"I've been wondering," Belle said. "BAMCorp gets its Fluinium from the belt asteroids. Why does the company need the deposits in this cave?"

Sasha pulled off her gloves and shook out her sweaty hands. "Mining asteroids is dangerous work. Several miners die on the job every cycle. If we can mine Fluinium on a stable planet, we could reduce the loss of life. Isn't that a worthy goal?"

Belle didn't know how to reply. Losing miners' lives was bad. But destroying the natural environment was too. She scratched the back of her neck. This was a difficult issue. Something didn't feel right to her, and she didn't quite know what it was. Sasha went back for more samples as Belle returned to her friends.

As the evening went on, more scientists arrived to help Sasha. They scraped samples off the cave walls. One scientist had an unusual tool that used a laser to pierce right through the cave floor. It made a narrow but deep hole.

A little later Sasha brought her datapad over to the others, and they spoke quietly to each other. Belle approached them to hear what they were saying, but they stopped speaking. The scientists looked at her curiously and then at Yixa, who was filming everything.

"How can BAMCorp just come here and decide to take over?" Belle asked. She had figured out what was bothering her. This cave didn't belong to the company. In a way, it belonged to everyone.

"BAMCorp owns the rights to all Fluinium deposits," Sasha said. "It always has."

Belle thought about that for a moment. "But you said the crater might have been formed millions of years ago."

"Maybe billions," Sasha said, nodding.

"So, are you saying that if a Fluinium-filled asteroid crashed onto a planet that wasn't colonized yet, BAMCorp already owns it? What if another species already lives there — can BAMCorp just claim it?"

"That can't be right," Ta'al added. "*Oodoxit* crash into planets all the time!"

"Yeah, that's not fair," Lucas added, joining in.

"And if BAMCorp owns the Fluinium, doesn't it mean they must only remove Fluinium?" Belle pressed on. "Can they do that without disturbing or harming the other elements present in the rocks? Surely BAMCorp isn't saying that it owns every planet that has the slightest bit of Fluinium?"

Belle knew she was babbling, but Sasha's statement really bothered her. She thought that BAMCorp was acting like her baby sister, Thea, who thought everything in the house was hers to play with.

"The child asks some good questions," Yixa said, hovering over the scientists. "Any comment?"

"I'm not a child," Belle insisted. "I'm fourteen."

Yixa blinked. "Sorry."

"I don't know the answers. I'm just a junior scientist," Sasha said. "We should go. There are too many people in here now." She gestured to Belle and her friends to leave ahead of her. Yixa followed them out.

Outside the cave stood Melody, Ms. Polley, and their entire class. Ms. Polley didn't look pleased.

"We've been looking for you three," their teacher said. She looked as if she'd been running a long distance. "We're heading out to Pettit. Melody has packed your things."

"Why?" Belle asked. "You said were staying."

"I recorded some holo-vids of the talks between BAMCorp and the curators," Melody said. "I showed them to your parents."

"We've been ordered to return home as soon as possible," Ms. Polley said. "Your parents are worried."

Belle wanted to argue, but she knew she'd lost this time. She trudged behind her class back toward their hover-wagon.

"What did you find out from the recordings?" she asked Melody.

"Only that both sides are very stubborn," Melody said.

"They are in negotiations," Ms. Polley added. "You remember what that is, right? You negotiated the visit to the desalination plant. This is a lot like that. Hopefully there will be a compromise."

Belle's heart sank. In her compromise, she didn't get to see as much of the desalination plant as she wanted. She'd enjoyed the sweet dessert, but she hadn't won. And in this case of BAMCorp versus the environment, the environment couldn't afford to lose, even a little. A compromise wouldn't necessarily be a good solution.

They exited the trail on the other side of the museum. As they headed back toward their campsite, Belle caught sight of Seb and Munny. She wanted to stop and say goodbye, but Ms. Polley kept marching the class away from the crowd. Belle tried to wave, but Seb and Munny were deep in discussions with the BAMCorp officials. They both looked upset. Seb was gesturing and waving his arms about angrily. Munny shook his head.

It looked like the environment was losing.

Belle was about to give up and follow her class when she saw Seb step up close to the tall BAMCorp rep.

She shoved him away. Munny caught Seb to keep him from falling over backward. Then the shorter rep clenched his fists and stepped in front of the taller one. He looked as if he might start throwing punches any second. Without thinking, Belle ran toward them. She didn't know what she could do, but she wanted to defend her new friends.

"Stop!" she cried as she squeezed her way between both parties. She held her arms out — as if she alone could stop them from fighting. For a second, the reps, Seb, and Munny looked confused. They stared down at her. "Fighting won't solve anything! Use your words, not your fists."

She was so scared that the words just tumbled out of her mouth. Only after she'd spoken did she realize she sounded just like her mother. Zara had always told her that talking things out produced more results than fighting. Her advice must have sunk in, after all this time.

"You are such a busybody, aren't you, little girl?" the tall rep snapped.

"Yeah," the other agreed. "Get out of our way."

"Hey! Leave the kid alone," Munny shouted. He yanked Belle behind him. "Belle, you shouldn't get involved here. It's too dangerous."

Seb grabbed her by the shoulders. "Get back to your teacher. We can take care of ourselves."

"But you can't win!" Belle exclaimed, tears beginning to flow. "BAMCorp already owns every speck of Fluinium."

The reps brushed themselves off and returned to confront the protestors. Seb and Munny stood side by side, blocking Belle behind them. More BAMCorp reps appeared from the land transports. Belle swallowed her tears. This was going to turn into a fight. And she was stuck in the middle of it.

How did she keep getting herself into these scrapes?

Belle heard a commotion. She turned around. Every protestor in the area was on their feet. They came to stand with Seb and Munny. They outnumbered the BAMCorp reps at least five to one. Emerging through the crowd, Melody came to Belle's side.

"We have to go, Belle," she said. "There is nothing more that you can do."

But Belle was too scared to move. She couldn't leave without knowing what would happen to her friends and the other protestors. She needed to see if BAMCorp would win. There was too much at stake.

Ju'arn weaved her way through the crowd and stood between the two sides. In her hands she held a holo-pad.

It showed the face of Secretary Sukanya, assistant to the Governor of Olympia. Ju'arn held up her free hand to get everyone's attention. "The Secretary wishes to speak," she said.

Secretary Sukanya's image stared out at the crowd. Her eyes landed on Belle. "Well, hello again," she said, recognizing Belle from the last time they'd met at the ancient site outside Sun City. "It seems whenever there's something interesting going on, I find you there, Miss Isabelle Song."

Belle shuffled her feet, and twisted her fingers together. This was her chance to do her part. She took a deep breath and spoke. "Please don't let BAMCorp take over here. People would lose too much. This planet is all we have for a home. Is getting rich with Fluinium more important than the environment?"

The smallest hint of a smile played on Secretary Sukanya's lips. "I had an interesting conversation with one of the scientists inside," she said. "She and I agree that you raised some very good questions about the ownership of Fluinium deposits. But I think it's time you let the authorities settle things. It is for your own safety, Belle."

"Come," Melody said, holding Belle by the arm. Seb and Munny nodded for her to go with her android.

Belle sighed. She'd done all she could. There was nothing left for her to do.

The Secretary turned to the crowd. "I have sent Protectors and drones to the scene. The negotiations and the collecting of samples have been suspended as of ten minutes ago. BAMCorp leaders have been called to appear before the Utopian authorities. The negotiations have been moved to the capital. I and other government representatives will meet with all sides in three days."

"We demand to be invited to that table," Seb said, refusing to back down.

Ju'arn bowed her head. "That was a condition that I requested with the Secretary."

Seb and Munny wove their hands in a dance-like movement. They thanked Ju'arn in the traditional Nabian way.

The BAMCorp reps soon returned to their transports, followed by the scientists and all their equipment. The Secretary said something to Ju'arn, and then her image fizzled out, just as the hum of drones filled the air above them.

The protestors cheered and clapped in triumph, and then began to leave. Seb and Munny turned to Belle with a relieved smile.

"But you didn't win," Belle said to them, disappointed.

"We live to fight another day," Munny said.

"And we couldn't have done it without you and your friends," Seb said. "So, thank you."

Belle wasn't satisfied with what had just happened. But she took comfort in knowing that, at least for today, the mountain and forests were safe. She said goodbye to Seb and Munny and wished them luck in the negotiations.

When she joined her classmates and teacher, Ms. Polley looked terrible. Her hair was mussed up and she had streaks of dirt all over her face.

"This has been the most eventful trip I've ever led," she said, rubbing her temples.

Belle felt sorry for her teacher, but these last few days had taught her more than she could ever learn in a classroom. Belle would never look at Mars and all that they had in the same way again.

Ms. Polley weaved a path between protestors heading out of the campground. They moved slowly because there were so many people. Melody insisted that everyone hold hands so they wouldn't lose each other.

"I am not going to search for you again," she told Belle and all her friends.

When they finally reached their hover-wagon, Ju'arn was standing in front of it, waiting for them.

"Traffic will be terrible now that everyone is leaving," she said to Ms. Polley. "Why don't you all come back to the museum for some refreshments? The Secretary has arranged for a special shuttle to take you all home from here later tonight."

"That is so generous," Ms. Polley said with a big smile.

"It's all because of Belle," Ava said. Everyone cheered.

"And maybe we can finish that tour, just like you promised," Belle said, blushing.

"Yeah!" her classmates agreed.

Ms. Polley brightened at the idea of refreshments. "I could use a break before the long flight," she said. "And I'd love to see that exhibit on the impact to the environment again."

Sol 50, Autumn/Cycle 106
Just past midnight.

Ju'arn was so nice to us. We got a private tour of the museum after she fed us yummy desserts and cold drinks. We had missed the exhibits earlier that showed all the different animals that lived in the forests. I'm so glad the mining plans have stopped — at least for now. So many animals would lose their homes if the forest were cut down. Then where would they go? If the animals moved into areas where people live, it wouldn't be good for any species.

The shuttle arrived for us a few hours later. It was a special private shuttle with just enough seats for us all. I'm seated in the back row with Ta'al and Ava. Lucas looked like he was going to sit with us, but then Ava squeezed her way in first — as usual.

Everyone else is asleep. We're all exhausted, but I can't stop thinking about everything that happened today. It's taking me longer to fall asleep. Writing helps me calm down.

I can't wait to tell Mom, Dad, and even Thea about all that's happened. And I intend to find a way to track the negotiations. The fight isn't over yet!

CHAPTER NINE
ENGAGING MARS' LEADERS

Three days later, Ta'al and Lucas came over to Belle's house to watch the news together. Today was the day. The negotiations that Secretary Sukanya had talked about were taking place that afternoon. RedVision was broadcasting the meeting live. Over the last few days, the situation with BAMCorp had become headline news. Everyone had an opinion, and each one was different from the next.

"I don't see Seb or Munny," Belle said, settling into the sofa with a cup of cocoa that Melody had made for them.

Her friends sat on either side of her. Lucas' leg bumped against Belle's, and for a moment she couldn't concentrate on what was being said on RedVision. Instead, all she could think about was how fast her heart was beating with Lucas sitting so close to her. She hadn't reacted to him like that before. What was wrong with her?

"You're right," Ta'al said, bringing Belle's attention back. "The Defenders of Olympus are not represented here. I see several other groups, but not Seb or Munny."

Lucas pulled up his datapad and searched for news about the DoO.

"Uh-oh," he said. "It says here that the leaders of the DoO have been arrested."

"What?" Belle jumped up. "Why?"

Lucas squinted at the screen. "It seems they organized a sit-in protest in front of the government building a day before the meeting. This went against their agreement with the company and government officials. When they refused to break up the protest, they were arrested."

"Oh no!" Belle couldn't believe it. Her friends were in prison? "We have to do something. But what?"

"What's wrong?" Yun walked into the living room at that moment. He pulled off his special gloves and peeled off the hat that kept him cool in the autumn heat.

Belle explained what she'd just learned about Seb and Munny. "How can we help them, Dad?"

Yun frowned and headed to the washroom to clean up. Belle looked at her friends, but neither of them had any ideas. A minute later, Yun popped back into the living room.

"I have an idea," he said. "You get along well with Secretary Sukanya. Why don't you send her a message expressing your concern? Appeal to her sense of justice. It's an old-fashioned way of engaging with our leaders, but it's worked before."

"*Mentisoi*! That's a great idea," Ta'al said. "My parents have done that in the past, and it seems to work."

"Let's get started then." Belle pulled out her datapad and her friends did the same. They looked up contact information for the Secretary, and sat around the dining table to compose their thoughts.

As they worked on what to say in their message, the doorbell rang. The rest of Belle's classmates stood outside.

"We saw that all the Defenders of Olympus have been told to leave the negotiations," Ava said.

"We thought we should do something to help them," Brill added.

"Perfect timing," Belle told them, ushering her classmates to the dining room. She told them what they were doing, and everyone got excited.

"We could each send our own message to the Secretary," Pavish said, taking out his datapad.

"What if we also send messages to other government leaders?" Lucas chimed in. "And maybe even to BAMCorp. They have a community feedback page right here." He pointed to the holo-screen with the giant BAMCorp logo in the background. "They claim to care about what we think."

"Then let's tell them," Ta'al said. "They should all know how concerned we are about the situation."

Everyone got to work. They discussed what they should say and how best to say it. As Mars' future generation, the students wanted their leaders to know how they felt about preserving the health of the environment and the planet. They also requested the release of Seb and Munny, who were only trying to make sure everyone had a future.

"I found a saying from Earth," Lucas said, squinting at his datapad. "It says, 'The Earth is not a gift passed to us from our parents. It is a loan from our children.' It's from a place called Kenya, back in the old days."

"We could adapt that for Mars," Belle said. She was glad they were all doing something to help their friends and to try to defend their home.

"When we're in school tomorrow," she continued, "we could get all of the classes involved. If we start spreading the message, it could get a lot of attention. And then BAMCorp would have to listen, right?"

"That's right," Yun said, emerging from the bedrooms with a sleepy Thea in his arms. "I'm proud of all of you kids. It's great that you're getting involved and doing your part for the planet."

Thea clapped and giggled.

"We want Mars to be as beautiful for Thea when she grows up, as it is today for us." Belle gave her baby sister a kiss.

"Sometimes, you surprise me, Belle," Yun said, hugging her around her shoulders. "You really aren't a kid anymore."

Belle rolled her eyes. "Dad, I've been telling you that for years."

When they finished their messages, they took turns recording them as holo-vids. They each sent their messages to as many official representatives as they could. As the last message was sent, Belle felt a great sense of accomplishment.

"I'd say we've done a great job," Lucas said.

"Too bad this whole thing interrupted our camping trip," Trina said.

"Maybe next fall we'll have an actual four-night trip," Brill said.

Belle looked at her friends. It really wasn't fair that their trip had been cut short. She felt partially responsible for that, since she was the one who fell and was poisoned by the Fluinium. None of this would've happened if she hadn't been so careless. But then she had a wonderful idea.

"Why don't we camp outside tonight? A group *matekap* — sleepover. We could do it here at our farm," she said. "It's not Mount Olympus, but we'll get to use our tents."

"I could cook over an open fire, just like at the campground," Melody added. She set a tray of cookies on the table for everyone.

"That's a wonderful idea," Ta'al said.

It was agreed that everyone would get their parents' permission and return that evening with their camping gear. They would set up camp under the giant apple trees at the edge of the Songs' farmland. Yun and Zara promised to leave them alone, as long as Melody was with them.

That night, as the sun set in the distance, Belle and her friends sat around a small fire that Melody built. She had done some research and found a special Earth dessert.

"I believe these are called Marsh-O-Mores," she said. She taught them how to toast marshmallows over the fire. Then she showed them how to assemble the marshmallows together with squares of chocolate and cookies. It was a sticky, gooey delight for all.

Belle finished her first one and was licking her lips when her dad approached.

"You promised to leave us alone," she whined.

Yun held his datapad in his hands. "You have a special call," he said. "It's the Secretary."

Belle felt bad for whining at her dad. She took his datapad and held the holo-display up against the night sky. The Secretary's head floated like an eerie ball.

"Miss Song," she began. "I wanted to thank you and your friends for the messages you sent today. Several of my colleagues received similar messages, and they wanted me to pass on their greetings. We are very pleased that so many young people are interested enough to get involved like this."

"We think our whole school might get involved," Belle said, licking the last of the chocolate off her lips. She told the Secretary of their plans.

"Good, good," she said. "The more messages we get from the community, the better. It will put pressure on all our leaders to do what the people want. And I assure you that we will do our best to preserve the delicate balance of nature on our planet. We have as much stake in this as you do. But keep engaging us in our work. It is our duty and privilege to hear from the people we represent."

"What about Seb and Munny, from the Defenders of Olympus?" Belle asked.

"They were released earlier this evening with a warning not to break the law again," Secretary Sukanya said. "They weren't going to be detained for long anyway. But there are proper ways to get your voice heard. I think you and your friends have demonstrated that well."

Belle nodded. "Thank you, Secretary." She held the holo-display toward all her friends, who waved and thanked the Secretary too.

"My office will keep you informed of our progress in the negotiations," the Secretary said. "One day, when you're older, you might want to consider serving as a leader in our community." She grinned at Belle and ended the chat. For a few seconds, Belle held the darkened datapad, and thought about the Secretary's words.

"Do you think you'd want to be a politician when you grow up, Belle?" Yun asked, taking back his datapad. "You've certainly had plenty of experience dealing with the authorities."

Belle looked at her dad and then back at her friends. They were busy making more Marsh-O-Mores by the fire and laughing loudly.

"I don't really know what I want to do when I'm an adult," she said. "Right now, I'm having too much fun just being a kid."

Sol 53, Autumn/Cycle 106
Late night.

We stayed up so late that I bet the sun is about to rise. Ta'al could barely keep her eyes open. But we had so much fun! Even Ava didn't complain.

Just before I snuggled into my sleeping bag, I got a short message from Seb and Munny. The Secretary was telling the truth. The guys were released from prison earlier today. Their records were cleared, as long as they promised to stay out of trouble. They said they were impressed that we flooded our leaders with messages. They promised to keep in touch.

I opened up the roof of our tent so we can see the stars outside. They're so pretty. Earth is a tiny bluish dot in the sky. I look at my old planet and wonder if we can take better care of Mars than we did Earth? I hope so. I hate to think that some family in the future will have to leave Mars to make a better life for themselves on another faraway planet. If they do leave, I hope they'll look back and see how beautiful Mars is and think about how much they'll miss it instead.

ABOUT THE AUTHOR

A.L. Collins learned a lot about writing from her teachers at Hamline University in St. Paul, MN. She has always loved reading science fiction stories about other worlds and strange aliens. She enjoys creating and writing about new worlds, as well as envisioning what the future might look like. Since writing the Redworld series, she has collected a map of Mars that hangs in her living room and a rotating model of the red planet, which sits on her desk. When not writing, Collins enjoys spending her spare time reading and playing board games with her family. She lives near Seattle, Washington with her husband and five dogs.

• • • • • • • •

ABOUT THE ILLUSTRATOR

Tomislav Tikulin was born in Zagreb, Croatia. Tikulin has extensive experience creating digital artwork for book covers, posters, DVD jackets, and production illustrations. Tomislav especially enjoys illustrating tales of science fiction, fantasy, and scary stories. His work has also appeared in magazines such as *Fantasy & Science Fiction*, *Asimov's Science Fiction*, *Orson Scott Card's Intergalactic Medicine Show*, and *Analog Science Fiction & Fact*. Tomislav is also proud to say that his artwork has graced the covers of many books including Larry Niven's *The Ringworld Engineers*, Arthur C. Clarke's *Rendezvous With Rama*, and Ray Bradbury's *Dandelion Wine* (50th anniversary edition).

:WHAT DO YOU THINK?:

1. Imagine you were part of Belle's class during their field trip. Write down the supplies that they should take along on a hike. What would you do if someone in the group was injured or lost on the mountain trail?

2. After meeting the leaders of the Defenders of Olympus, Belle and her friends decided to join the protesters. Do you think this was the best way to show their feelings and beliefs about the environment? What do you think they would do if the protest became violent?

3. If you were a Martian reporter, what questions would you want to ask the BAMCorp officials, Secretary Sukanya, the museum curators, or Belle and her friends? Write out the interview as a news report.

4. Belle, Ta'al, and Lucas decided to go back to the cave with the reporter and scientist. But they didn't wait for Melody or ask their teacher for permission to do so. Do you think this was wise? Why or why not? How do you think Ms. Polley felt when she found them back at the cave?

5. Belle and her friends sent messages to government and BAMCorp officials to express their concerns for the environment. Think about what they would want to tell the officials, and then write down a message in their words.

:GLOSSARY:

antidote (AN-ti-dote) — something that stops a poison from working

curator (KYOO-ray-tur) — a person who is in charge of a place that displays exhibits, such as a museum

desalination (dee-sah-luh-NAY-shuhn) — the process of removing salt from ocean water to purify it

element (EL-uh-muhnt) — a basic substance that cannot be broken down into simpler substances

fluorescent (flu-RESS-uhnt) — the quality of giving off bright light by using ultraviolet light or X-rays

integrate (IN-tuh-grate) — to bring people of different races together into one community

isolation (eye-suh-LAY-shuhn) — the condition of being alone

negotiation (ni-GOH-shee-ay-shuhn) — discussion between two opposing sides to reach an agreement

radioactive (ray-dee-oh-AK-tiv) — having to do with materials that give off potentially harmful invisible rays or particles

toxin (TOK-sin) — a poisonous substance

terraform (TER-uh-form) — to change the environment of a planet or moon to make it capable of supporting life

‌MARS TERMS‌

caluk (KAL-uhk) — Nabian word meaning "wait"

holo-vid (HOHL-uh-vid) — a holographic projection that shows videos for information or entertainment

Mars Cycle (MARS SY-kuhl) — the Martian year, equal to 687 Earth days, or 1.9 Earth years

matekap (MAH-the-kap) — Nabian word meaning "sleepover"

melyanti (mel-YAN-tye) — Nabian word meaning "fine"

mentisoi (men-tih-SOY) — Nabian meaning "brilliant"

Nabian (NAY-bee-uhn) — an advanced alien race with nose ridges and plastic-like hair; their eye color reflects their surroundings

oodoxit (OO-dock-sit) — Nabian word meaning "asteroid"

Sia-mi, sia carnti (SEE-ah-MEE SEE-uh karn-TIE) — Nabian words meaning "Thank you, my friend."

sia toh follari (SEE-ah TOE FOH-lahr-ee) — Nabian words meaning "that's right"

sol (SOHL) — the name for the Martian day

suemi (SWAY-mee) — Nabian word meaning "delicious"

Sulux (SUH-lux) — an alien race with purple skin and arm and neck ridges

svo tenya reyal (SVOH TEN-ya ray-ALL) — Nabian words meaning "you don't look right"

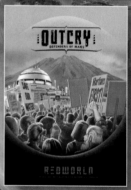

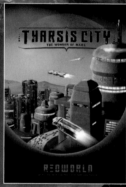